Do you know what my favorite part of the game is?
The opportunity to play.

– Mike Singletary

Kane Miller, A Division of EDC Publishing

Text and illustrations copyright © Richard Torrey 2012

All rights reserved.
For information contact:
Kane Miller, A Division of EDC Publishing
PO Box 470663
Tulsa, OK 74147-0663
www.kanemiller.com
www.edcpub.com

Library of Congress Control Number: 2011942607

Printed and bound in the United States of America

ISBN: 978-1-61067-163-7

1 2 3 4 5 6 7 8 9 10

A LITTLE BROWNS FOOTBALL Story

By Richard Torrey

Kane Miller
A DIVISION OF EDC PUBLISHING

This is my football.

My dad and I like to practice with it in the park. (It's my favorite thing to do.)

He teaches me about throwing ...

... and catching ...

... and running.

We always have the best time.

But today we're not going to the park.
That's because today I have my first real football practice,
with a real football team, that plays on a real football field.

The team gives everyone real football equipment to wear, so we don't get hurt.

Real football players wear football pants with lots of pads in them ...

... and shoulder pads.

Our coach is really nice, and he's tall.He also knows how to whistle really loud with just his mouth (not a whistle).

Coach tells us to jog all the way around the football field to warm up. Jogging is like running, only you don't try your hardest.

Next, we make a big circle around Coach.
He shows us how to stretch our muscles.

There is a lot we have to learn to get ready for our first real football game.

Coach teaches us how to hold a football with two hands, so we don't lose it when we run. When that happens, it's called a fumble.

We learn the right way to throw and catch the football.

We learn how to block.

And we learn how to tackle.

After that, we all get a drink of water.

Then Coach says it's time to scrimmage. A scrimmage is a practice football game where you don't have to keep score.

In the scrimmage, sometimes I get to tackle.

Sometimes I get to block.

And sometimes I get to carry the ball.

At the end of practice, Coach says now that we're on a real football team, we need to eat healthy foods and get plenty of sleep.

That's what real football players do, and I'm a real football player.

I think I'm going to like playing on a real football team.
But I still want to keep practicing with my dad.

Because now there are a lot of things I have to teach him.